The Story Book Prince

by
JOANNE OPPENHEIM

Illustrated by
ROSANNE LITZINGER

GULLIVER BOOKS/HARCOURT BRACE JOVANOVICH
San Diego   Austin   Orlando

Requests for permission to make copies of any
part of the work should be mailed to:
Permissions, Harcourt Brace Jovanovich, Publishers,
Orlando, Florida 32887.

Library of Congress Cataloging-in-Publication Data
Oppenheim, Joanne.
The story book prince.
Summary: No one can succeed in making the young
prince go to sleep, until an old woman tries with a
bedtime story.
[1. Bedtime—Fiction. 2. Sleep—Fiction.
3. Stories in rhyme] I. Litzinger, Rosanne, ill.
II. Title.
PZ8.3.0'0615St 1987   [E]   85-31745
ISBN 0-15-200590-0

Printed in Hong Kong
First edition   A B C D E

TO STEPHANIE AND HER PRINCE CHARMING
—J.O.

FOR DONNA, JOHN, AND CHRIS
WITH LOVE
—R.L.

In a faraway kingdom, a long time ago,
when bedtime came the Prince said, "No!"

The Queen tucked her son in a quilt made of silk.
The cook brought him cookies. The maid brought hot milk.
Though everyone tried to make the Prince sleep,
the harder they tried, the more he would weep.

"This cannot go on," said the King. "I am sure
that somebody somewhere knows some sort of cure!"

So the next day he sent forth a royal request
to the north, to the south, to the east, and the west:

IF ANYONE KNOWS HOW TO MAKE THE PRINCE REST
PLEASE COME AT ONCE TO THE ROYAL ADDRESS!

The first to arrive was a bearded Physician
who promised his tonic would cure the condition.

The prince closed his lips as tight as could be.
"It's good," said his mother. "Taste it and see."
But the Prince shook his head and pulled up the cover.
"Watch," said the Doctor, "I'll give some to your mother."

The Queen took a spoonful, crooning "m-m-m" sweetly.
"Delicious!" She yawned, and was instantly sleepy.

The court then followed their Queen's fine example.
They each took one sip, and that one sip was ample.

Licking their lips, murmuring "m-m-m, it's sweet!"
Then, quick as a wink they all fell asleep. . . .

Except for the Prince, who heard them all snoring
and said with disgust, "How perfectly boring!"

The next night five dancers arrived with musicians.
"We'll dance 'til he's tired—come, take your positions."
The signal was given, the dancing began.
Some say they danced, but really they ran.
Around in a circle, first left and then right.
They whirled and they twirled well into the night.

They danced through the castle 'til quarter past four,
When the King cried, "Enough! My feet are too sore!"

Then all of them groaned and collapsed on the floor,
except for the Prince, who begged, "Let's dance some more!"

The next to arrive at the old castle gate
Was a mustached magician in high hat and cape.
"Your Grace," he said, "with your kind permission,
my hypnotic spells can cure this condition."

"Proceed." The King yawned. "Do what you can."
"I'll start with some tricks," the magician began.
With a wave of the hand and a whisper of words
he brought forth from nowhere a flurry of birds,
a bouquet of posies, a rabbit of course,
and last but not least, he brought forth a horse!

"A horse in the castle!" the Queen screamed. "No more!"
"Guards!" called the King, "show him the door!"

"Oh, why?" the Prince cried.
"Can't I take a ride?"

The next night at bedtime the Prince got a present.
A featherdown quilt stuffed with feathers of pheasant.
"Sire," said the peasant who brought him the present,
"the Prince cannot sleep in a bed that's unpleasant.

Try this, little Prince, it's soft as new snow.
You'll drift off to dreamland. You'll love it, I know."

The prince was so happy he jumped in head first.
He jumped in so hard . . . the featherbed burst.

"ACHOO!" wheezed the King.
"ACHOO!" sneezed the Queen.
It took them 'til morning to get the place clean.

But the Prince was so tickled he giggled all night:
"I've never ever seen such a truly silly sight!"

Night after night they tried to amuse him.
Night after night there was endless confusion.
Jugglers tried juggling. Jesters made gestures.
Learned professors made countless conjectures.
Nurse sang lullabies. Cook baked cake.
But alas the small Prince still stayed wide awake.

Then one night past bedtime—it was long after eight—
An old woman came to the great palace gate.

"Your Majesties, please"—she curtsied quite low—
"I'll get him to sleep if you'll just stop this show."

"And what do you do? Do you dance? Can you sing?
What's in your bag? What did you bring?"

"Of course I can dance, and I do love to sing.
But for bedtime," she said, "I've the very best thing."
Reaching into her bag she pulled out a book,
and said to the Prince, "I'll read while you look."

"In a faraway kingdom a long time ago,
when bedtime came the Prince said, 'No!'"

"But where are the pictures?" asked the Prince in surprise.
"You'll see them," she said, "if you just close your eyes."

So that's what he did. He shut his eyes tight.
And soon after that . . . fell asleep for the night.

The full color artwork in this book was done on 147 lb. Fabriano watercolor paper using brown ink and painted with transparent watercolor dyes and opaque tempera.

The text type was set via the Linotron 202 in Weiss.

The display type was set in ITC Barcelona Book Italic.

Composition by Thompson Type, San Diego, California.

Printed and bound by South China Printing Company, Quarry Bay, Hong Kong.

Production supervision by Warren Wallerstein and Eileen McGlone.

Designed by Joy Chu